Morgan Makes Magic

Ted Staunton

Morgan Makes Magic

Illustrations by Bill Slavin

FIRST NOVELS

The New Series

Formac Publishing Limited
Halifax, Nova Scotia

Formac Publishing Company Limited acknowledges the
support of The Canada Council and the Nova Scotia Depart-
ment of Education and Culture in the development of writing
and publishing in Canada.

Canadian Cataloguing in Publication Data

Staunton, Ted, 1956-

   Morgan makes magic

   (First novel series)

ISBN 0-88780-390-3 (pbk)   ISBN 0-88780-391-1 (bound)

I.Slavin, Bill. II. Title. III. Series.

PS8587.T334M67 1997   jC813'.54   C96-950187-0
PZ7.S8076Mo 1997

Formac Publishing Limited
5502 Atlantic Street
Halifax, NS B3H 1G4

Printed and bound in Canada.

Table of Contents

1
Hummel the Bummel

It's ten minutes to nine, my first day at my new school. I've got on new everything, even new underwear. I might as well have a sign that says: MORGAN— NEW KID. I feel like a new bozo.

Really, I want my old stuff with my old friends at my old school, but I'm trying not to think about that. Instead, I'm watching these kids play ball and hoping for someone to talk to. I'm not so great at sports, but I'm a pretty good talker.

The thing is, everybody just zooms right by. Maybe something weird in my new clothes has made me invisible. But wait: a girl is running this way. She looks like a popsicle stick in a purple sweatsuit.

"Hummel the Bummel!" the kids yell. "Give it back, Aldeen!"

Now I see she's grabbed the ball from the game.

"No way, nerd-brains!" she shrieks. She has a laugh like a hyena.

She aims for the roof but she can't throw for beans—worse than me, even. The ball bonks the wall and bounces past me into a hole with an iron grating over it. Everybody stomps over.

It's my chance. I smile and

point. "It went in there." My face feels like a hot potato. The girl called Aldeen glares at me. My face gets hotter. Everyone else bends over the grating.

"Get it, Matt."

"It's too far. Ky–le, *move*!"

"I can't. I think I'm stuck."

A crowd gathers. A teacher comes over. The girl smiles as if she's saving a stink bomb for

later. When the bell goes, she bumps into me on purpose as she runs by. "Out of the way, tubbo."

Something turns sour inside of me. When I get to my new class I see a purple popsicle stick back. Aldeen Hummel sits right in front of me.

2
Telling Tales

Did I say Aldeen Hummel has witchy hair? Well, she does. I've looked at it all week, so I know. She also has about three thousand ways to bug everybody. On Tuesday it was sneaky pinches. Thursday she shut down the computers. At Friday recess she held up four classes tying her shoes on the stairs, then hogged the fountain.

Now it's Saturday. I'm sitting up in the playfort the last people built in our back yard. It's cool. There's an orange roof, a rope ladder, a slide, a tire swing. This

thing would practically be worth moving for—if there was someone to share it with. On my old street you knew everybody from when you were born, practically. You didn't have to *make* friends, they'd just always been there.

"It'll get better, Morgan," my parents say. Maybe. Everybody likes my goofy voices, but I stink at soccer and I've got this flat tire feeling there's no room for me. Yesterday I asked Charlie, who sits beside me, if he could come over. He was going to Adair's house. Will was going to Ian's. A.J. was going to Mark's.

"That's okay," I said to Charlie. "I have my bass guitar lesson."

"I forgot, I have to go to karate later anyway," I told Will.

"No sweat," I said to A.J. "I've gotta practise juggling."

Then I came home and watched TV.

Now I look around the playfort and wonder what to do. At least there's no Aldeen.

"Morgan," my mom calls from the house. "Telephone."

If it's one of the guys from my old street I'll tell him I have to go to two birthday parties this afternoon. I pick up the phone.

"Hi Morgan," Charlie says. "Want to come over?"

3
Too Excellent

"What took you?" Charlie asks when I get to his place. I didn't notice before, but he has these braces on his teeth. Charlie doesn't talk much.

"I had to finish fixing our car," I say before I even think about it. Really I had to help with the dishes, but what if Charlie thinks that's dumb?

Charlie has about six tons of space Lego. He also has a whole shelf full of sports trophies. They make me nervous. I hoist my jeans up higher over my bum so I'll maybe look thinner, and as we play I say, "It's lucky for me you called. I was gonna have to practise drums all afternoon."

"I thought you played the bass guitar," Charlie says.

"Oh, that too," I say very fast, and pretend to hunt for a Lego piece. Was that what I told him? I can't remember.

"A.J. says you can juggle, too."

"Some," I say carefully. "But I'm better at magic tricks. My dad taught me; he's in the circus."

"*Cool*!" Charlie says. "Want to go outside and play hockey?"

We take turns being goalie. I'm crummy at hockey, but I kind of fill up the net. Charlie cleans me anyway. I don't mind; Charlie is a good guy. Of course

I can't let him meet my dad, who has never been in the circus. Maybe I'm *too* excellent at talking.

But hey, what's wrong with that?

4
Attack of the Purple Popsicle

I'll tell you what's wrong with that: EVERYTHING.

Here's what happened. At lunch on Wednesday it was raining. I was sitting with Charlie and A.J. and Matt. Aldeen Hummel was sitting by herself at the same table because no one ever wants to sit beside her. "Hey, Jessica," she was yelling, "I put big grey boogers in your sandwich." She'd been a real pain all morning, mixing up everybody's boots.

"Geez," Matt said, "I wish we could play a game outside." I

was kind of glad we didn't have to. Then I saw the dime on the table. I remembered a game from my old school, one I was even good at.

"Hey," I said, "finger hockey!"

"Huh?" everybody said.

"I'll show you. Gimme two more dimes." I shook the money in my hands like an expert pro and dumped it on the table.

"Okay, Charlie, hook your little finger and your first finger onto the table top. That's the net. Now watch. You have to flick one dime between the other two every time to work across the table and take a shot."

I got my flicking finger ready and WHAM! something slammed the table. The dimes hopped into the air. So did I.

"GAAH!" I shouted and whipped around. Aldeen Hummel's popsicle stick fist was still on the table.

"Hey, Tub-ola!" she yelled. "That's my dime."

5
Finger Hockey Hero

Before I could say anything, Charlie said, "Get lost, Aldeen."

"Shut up, zippermouth, I'm talking to him." Charlie's face got red. Aldeen turned to me.

"Give it," she said, "NOW."

She looked like Godzilla, but right then I was so mad at her for spoiling my game I didn't care. I scooped up one of the dimes and said, "Watch, Aldeen: magic." Then I pretended to take it out of my hand and rub it against my elbow. Really, I left the dime in my palm and dropped it down the back of my shirt, but when I lifted my rubbing hand off my sleeve it looked like the dime had vanished. It's the only trick I know.

Aldeen was so stunned, her teeth practically fell out. For one microsecond I thought she was going to cry. Then Godzilla was back.

"Give it!" she yelled again.

"I can't," I teased her. "It's gone."

Really, I was already reaching behind my back to get it out, but before I could, she roared, "I'm gonna get you," grabbed her lunch bag and stomped out.

There was total silence, then everybody cheered at once.

"Morgan got Aldeen!"

"Hummel the Bummel gets burned!"

They pounded me on the back so much the dime dropped down my pants. I grinned, but I wasn't as happy as they were. I mean, Aldeen hadn't said she was going to get *them*, had she?

6
The Mouth Trap

So now I'm a star. Except, who wants to be? Aldeen is out to get me and I feel like a phoney baloney. After the way I did magic, everyone believes in all those stories I told. The thing is, now they want me to do them.

Matt and Ian both want to come over. It would be cool to show them the playfort, but what if they ask to see my bass guitar or the chemistry lab I don't really have? I tell them my dad needs things private to practise his tightrope walking.

Mark wants me to come to his house and do karate on his big brother, who's bugging him. I say it's against the law for karate guys to just go around breaking boards whenever they feel like it, in case people get hurt.

But now, worst of all, A.J. and Sherry and Ashley want me to juggle at recess! Did I say I could juggle? Dumb, dumb, dumb!

"My hand is too sore today from breaking boards," I say. "Maybe on Monday." Maybe they'll forget.

But as I turn around there's Aldeen staring at me, her eyes all narrow under her witchy hair. Was she listening? That gives me a feeling so creepy my

toes curl up in my sneakers. I decide to do something, fast. I reach in my pocket.

"Hey, Aldeen, here's your dime back."

She snatches it. "You're gonna be sorry anyway," she says.

7
Boink, Boink, Boink

At supper that night, I decide to skip my broccoli to save room for dessert. I also complain about Aldeen.

"She's always bugging everybody and getting in trouble. Plus she looks weird. She's crazy."

"She sounds more unhappy than crazy," my dad says.

"Ha," I snort, remembering that hyena laugh.

"Yogurt for dessert," says my mom. I eat my broccoli.

I go to the library and get a book on juggling, just in case. It doesn't help. On Monday, I

shuffle to school as late as I can, but Aldeen is waiting. "Think fast!" she yells and tosses me an apple. I catch it.

"Hey, everybody, Morgan's hand is better. He can juggle at recess!"

By recess the whole class is excited, except for me. I'm mush. Everyone gathers by the swings. Aldeen shoves three tennis balls at me. She's grinning like a crocodile. I wipe my hands on my shirt. I remember what the juggling book says. I clamp my tongue in my teeth, toss the balls in the air—and they drop like rocks: boink, boink, boink. I don't even catch one.

At first nobody says anything. Then someone snickers. There's

a laugh. Then everyone is laughing and I hear, "Bet he can't do karate either."

Then Charlie speaks. Charlie, who practically never talks. "Just wait," he says. "Tomorrow he'll do real magic."

8
Orange Blues

I'm sitting in the playfort by myself. The roof makes everything look orange, like barbeque potato chips. I don't care; I'm so worried I'm not even hungry. I know he didn't mean to, but why did Charlie have to make things worse? I look around at the rope ladder, the slide, the tire swing. Tomorrow even Charlie will find out I don't know magic. Nobody will come over after that.

Unless...I think for a long time, trying to find another way. There isn't one. Slowly I let down the rope ladder, go in the house and dial the phone.

"Hi, Charlie," I say, "want to come over?"

Charlie thinks the playfort is cool. He's on the tire swing when I say, looking the other way, "Hey Charlie, know how I can't juggle? I can't play the bass guitar either."

"Uh-huh." Charlie keeps swinging.

"And I don't know karate and I wasn't in a movie."

"Oh." Now Charlie is scampering up the rope ladder. "Hey, *cool*!" he says from up in the fort.

"There's no circus. My dad works for the phone company," I shout.

Charlie doesn't answer. I climb up.

"Are you mad?" I ask.

Charlie shrugs. He looks orange. "Nah. I didn't think you did *all* that stuff."

"But I lied. I can't do any of it."

"You sure can tell stories, though," Charlie says. "That's good." He gets on the slide. "This is neat too."

"But Charlie, I can't do magic! What am I gonna do about Aldeen?"

"You fooled her before," Charlie says. "Anybody that tells stories like you can think of something."

"Well," I say, "there's magic books at the library."

"So let's go." He zips down the slide. I follow. I think I've just made a friend.

9
The Perfect Trick

Charlie and I have found the perfect trick. I've already fooled Charlie's older brother with it, and my dad. It's perfect.

There's a tray with a piece of white paper on it, a dime, and a glass turned upside down. With everyone watching, I will bet Aldeen that I can make her dime disappear again. I'll put it on the paper, slide the glass over it and the dime will vanish! She will have a hairy fit and then I'll slide the glass back and there will be the money. Amazing or what, eh?

See, the trick is that there is a circle of white paper glued to the rim of the glass. As long as you don't lift the glass you can't see it, but it covers up the dime!

Anyway, that's not the important part. The important part is that tomorrow me and my buddy Charlie are going to cream Aldeen.

"Hummel the Bummel," I say to myself, "will look like a crummel."

I can hardly wait.

10
Real Magic

I get to school so early it's three days till the bell. There's no one else around. Everything is ready in my backpack, but something bugs me.

What if tricking Aldeen back makes us at war? I remember Aldeen in gym, trying to do headstands until her face turned purple. She just wouldn't give up. The thought makes my neck prickle, but I'm not chickening out. No way. I know I can trick her.

Now I see Aldeen at the corner. She's dawdling. I've never

seen a slow Aldeen before. Her hair is even witchier than usual and her runners are untied. She's wearing her purple sweat suit, but she doesn't even look as big as a popsicle stick today.

Does she always come to school this early? I slip behind the slide. Aldeen doesn't see me. She's eating a chocolate bar. At breakfast? She sits down on the steps in the empty schoolyard. I remember me sitting in my playfort. I don't want to remember. How come Aldeen is always by herself, I ask myself instead. That's easy: because she's a jerk. It's her own fault. I squirm some more. Anyway, that's not it. I guess what I mean is, how come Al-

deen Hummel is the way she is?

Who knows? My brain feels upside down. Except for one idea. I don't even want to think it, but it won't go away.

I'm still thinking it. It's telling me to try something scary. Now I don't know what to do. The school yard is starting to fill up. Soon it will be time. Is Charlie here yet? I have to change the plan. I don't want to, but I have to.

I have to. I run over to Aldeen. She looks up, surprised. Her eyes get squinty when she sees it's me. I get out the magic stuff. I don't say anything. She looks confused, and right then I know I can fool her. She knows it too, and as she starts to turn into Godzilla, I lift the glass so she can see the paper glued to it. I take a breath so deep it's bottomless and I say, "It's a new trick, Aldeen. Want to see how to do it?"

Meet five other great kids in the New First Novels Series:

- **Meet Duff the Daring**
  in *Duff the Giant Killer*
  by Budge Wilson/Illustrated by Kim LaFave
  Getting over the chicken pox can be boring, but Duff and Simon find a great way to enjoy themselves — acting out one of their favourite stories, *Jack the Giant Killer*, in the park. In fact, they do it so well the police get into the act.

- **Meet Jan the Curious**
  in *Jan's Big Bang*
  by Monica Hughes/Illustrated by Carlos Friere
  Taking part in the Science Fair is a big deal for Grade Three kids, but Jan and her best friend Sarah are ready for the challenge. Still, finding a safe project isn't easy, and the girls discover that getting ready for the fair can cause a whole lot of trouble.

- **Meet Robyn the Dreamer**
  in *Shoot for the Moon, Robyn*
  by Hazel Hutchins/ Illustrated by Yvonne Cathcart
  When the teacher asks her to sing for the class, Robyn knows it's her chance to be

the world's best singer. Should she perform like Celine Dion, or do *My Bonnie Lies Over the Ocean*, or the matchmaker song? It's hard to decide, even for the world's best singer — and the three boys who throw spitballs don't make it any easier.

• Meet Carrie the Courageous
in *Go For It, Carrie*
by Lesley Choyce/ Illustrated by Mark Thurman
More than anything else, Carrie wants to roller-blade. Her big brother and his friend just laugh at her. But Carrie knows she can do it if she just keeps trying. As her friend Gregory tells her, "You can do it, Carrie. Go for it!"

• Meet Lilly the Bossy
in *Lilly to the Rescue*
by Brenda Bellingham/ Illustrated by Kathy Kaulbach
Bossy-boots! That's what kids at school start calling Lilly when she gives a lot of advice that's not wanted. Lilly can't help telling people what to do — but how can she keep any of her friends if she always knows better?

Look for these First Novels!

- *About Arthur*
  Arthur Throws a Tantrum
  Arthur's Dad
  Arthur's Problem Puppy

- *About Fred*
  Fred and the Stinky Cheese
  Fred's Dream Cat

- *About the Loonies*
  Loonie Summer
  The Loonies Arrive

- *About Maddie*
  Maddie in Hospital
  Maddie Goes to Paris
  Maddie in Danger
  Maddie in Goal
  Maddie Wants Music
  That's Enough Maddie!

- *About Mikey*
  Good For You, Mikey Mite!
  Mikey Mite Goes to School
  Mikey Mite's Big Problem

- *About Mooch*
  Mooch Forever
  Hang On, Mooch!
  Mooch Gets Jealous
  Mooch and Me

- *About the Swank Twins*
  The Swank Prank
  Swank Talk

- *About Max*
  Max the Superhero

Formac Publishing Company Limited
5502 Atlantic Street, Halifax, Nova Scotia B3H 1G4
Orders: 1-800-565-1975 Fax: (902) 425-0166